Dear Parent:
Your child's love of reading starts here!

Every child learns to read in a different way and at his or her own speed. Some go back and forth between reading levels and read favorite books again and again. Others read through each level in order. You can help your young reader improve and become more confident by encouraging his or her own interests and abilities. From books your child reads with you to the first books he or she reads alone, there are I Can Read Books for every stage of reading:

SHARED READING
Basic language, word repetition, and whimsical illustrations, ideal for sharing with your emergent reader

BEGINNING READING
Short sentences, familiar words, and simple concepts for children eager to read on their own

READING WITH HELP
Engaging stories, longer sentences, and language play for developing readers

READING ALONE
Complex plots, challenging vocabulary, and high-interest topics for the independent reader

ADVANCED READING
Short paragraphs, chapters, and exciting themes for the perfect bridge to chapter books

I Can Read Books have introduced children to the joy of reading since 1957. Featuring award-winning authors and illustrators and a fabulous cast of beloved characters, I Can Read Books set the standard for beginning readers.

A lifetime of discovery begins with the magical words "I Can Read!"

Visit www.icanread.com for information
on enriching your child's reading experience.

For Orange Kitty
With love, SW

For my Mac, Tim
Love, Janie

I Can Read Book® is a trademark of HarperCollins Publishers.

Mac and Cheese and the Perfect Plan
Text copyright © 2012 by Sarah Weeks
Illustrations copyright © 2012 by Jane Manning
Library of Congress Cataloging-in-Publication Data
Weeks, Sarah.
    Mac and Cheese and the perfect plan / by Sarah Weeks ; illustrated by Jane Manning. — 1st ed.
       p.   cm. — (I can read. Level 1)
    Summary: Alley cat best friends come up with the perfect way to spend the day, even though they miss the bus to the beach.
    ISBN 978-0-06-117082-9 (trade bdg.) — ISBN 978-0-06-117084-3 (pbk.)
    [1. Stories in rhyme.   2. Best friends—Fiction.   3. Friendship—Fiction.   4. Cats—Fiction.]   I. Manning, Jane, date,
ill.   II. Title.
PZ8.3.W4125Mae 2010
[E]—dc22

2009001401
CIP
AC

20 21 LSCC 15 ❖   First Edition

MAC AND CHEESE
and the Perfect Plan

BY **Sarah Weeks**

ILLUSTRATED BY **Jane Manning**

HARPER
An Imprint of HarperCollins*Publishers*

Cheese is sleeping on his can.

"Wake up!" cries Mac. "I have a plan.

A perfect plan for you and me.

Wake up! We're going to the sea."

Cheese says, "A perfect plan, you say?
A perfect way to spend the day?"
He frowns at Mac and shakes his head
and says, "I plan to stay in bed."

"Get up!" cries Mac. "It's hot outside.

So hot we need to take a ride.

The bus will take us to the sea.

Get up now, Cheese, and come with me!"

"I do not like the sea," says Cheese.

"The sea is worse than having fleas.

The sand is hot, the wind will blow.

Forget it, Mac. I will not go."

Cheese is a very grumpy cat,

and Mac is not at all like that.

But Mac wants Cheese to come along

and so he sings this little song:

"Please, Cheese, please,

Come to the sea,

Come to the sea, Cheese,

Please with me."

Cheese does not like it when Mac sings.

(Cheese does not like a lot of things.)

He frowns and shakes his head, and then

Mac sings his little song again.

"Please, Cheese, please,

Come to the sea,

Come to the sea, Cheese,

Please with me."

Cheese shuts his two eyes very tight

and plugs his ears with all his might.

But even when he plugs his ears,

Mac's little song is all he hears.

"Stop!" cries Cheese. "Don't sing that song.

Don't sing and I will come along.

I'll ride the bus down to the sea.

Just please, please, please

don't sing to me."

15

"I will not sing one note," says Mac.

"You sit there, Cheese, and I'll go pack."

When Mac comes back, Cheese says,

"Oh dear.

There is not any milk in here."

Mac says, "I'll get some milk for you."

Cheese says, "Let's take some crackers, too."

Cheese also wants to take a hat,
some flip-flops, and a little mat.

A ring.   A rake.

A fan.   A cake.

A pail.   A cup.

Mac packs it up.

A kite.

A dish.

A chair.

A fish.

A clock.

A ball.

Mac packs it all.

Cheese says, "I'll need some books to read, and bring a boat so I can float."

Mac packs and packs, and when he's done,
Cheese sees the bus. "Mac, hurry, run!"

Slip!

Trip!

Rip!

There goes the ring, there goes the mat.

There goes the milk, there goes the hat.

There goes the boat, there goes the cake.

There goes the fan, there goes the rake.

Mac starts to cry. "Please, wait for us!"

Oh no! Oh no!

There goes . . .

the bus.

Cheese says, "Don't cry, Mac.

Close your eyes.

You're going to get a big surprise!

I've got a perfect plan now too.

We can't go to the sea, it's true,

So . . .

I will bring the sea to you!"

Mac is so glad, he starts to sing.

And Cheese does not say anything.